Forever and Always

A WIDOW'S RECOLLECTION OF
LIFE, LOSS AND LOVE

Melissa Simmons

Forever and Always

A Widow's Recollection of

Life, Loss, and Love

© Copyright 2014. Melissa Simmons. All Rights Reserved

ISBN: 1502768593
ISBN 13: 9781502768599
Library of Congress Control Number: 2014918220
CreateSpace Independent Publishing Platform
North Charleston, South Carolina

Contents

A Special Thank-You	ix
Foreword	xi
Chapter 1 A Widow's Prison	1
Chapter 2 Love in a Stranger's Kitchen	6
Chapter 3 Watching for Signs	12
Chapter 4 "Daddy"	21
Chapter 5 Another Reason to Smile	25

Chapter 6
    Sharing Parenthood   29

Chapter 7
    Without Him   33

Chapter 8
    "Home"   41

Chapter 9
    Living Life to Its Fullest   51

Chapter 10
    Every Step of the Way   57

Chapter 11
    She Would Overcome   61

Chapter 12
    Just His Way   66

Chapter 13
    A Love Like No Other   69

Chapter 14
    Open Arms   74

A Note from the Author	**79**
Conclusion	**81**
The Five Stages of Grief	81
About the Author	**87**

A Special Thank-You

It is with mixed emotions that I give acknowledgment to the man who made this book possible. Andy, without your undying love and persuasion both in life and even in death, I would never have found the courage not only to recognize but to achieve this dream. I only wish you had been here to share this joy with me.

I would also like to thank my family and friends for understanding my need to at times put up what may have seemed like walls and also for their faith in our relationships to have the strength to reach out and bust through them when I got too "pulled in" to realize.

Words cannot even express my gratitude toward the people who joined my world when Andy could no longer reside here. Without your love and support, this project would have never taken flight. This includes, although not exclusively, the friends whom I've never met face to face. Your belief in my (and Andy's dream) is overwhelming—and oftentimes a driving force for me.

Melissa Simmons

To those of you who took time out of your busy lives to proofread and edit these words, my feelings of gratitude for your help cannot even begin to be expressed.

I present this book in honor of
my one true love.
Andy, may you rest in peace—until I get there! (Wink, wink!)
Gone but not forgotten!
Forever and always, baby!
In loving memory of my one and only,
Andy Simmons,
1961–2012.

Foreword

Sometimes it is necessary to look back at the past in order to see how far we've come. I realized that this morning at 4:00 a.m. when I stepped out to beat the heat, while attempting to get in my usual four miles of walking.

The dimly lit starry sky, smell of the neighborhood farm animals, and freshly cut hay, as well as other natural aromas prevalent in the country were my only guides. The sounds of the locusts and crickets would be my entertainment. The scent of a lingering skunk crossed my path at one point, warning me to reconsider taking my normal route.

I began walking as a form of therapy whenever words seemed to fail. An inspiration can appear from almost anything, it seems, and today mine came from my worn out tennis shoes.

I remember the day they came into my life four years ago. I was working a job that required a lot of walking and standing. I was already suffering from tremendous back pain after being involved in an automobile accident nearly eight years before, and while I tried to deny the fact, I knew that it would eventually require surgery. So I took a chunk of change and dropped it on a pair of decent but not overly priced walking shoes. Five months later, they would be put on sabbatical as I underwent major surgery.

It seemed that my back had finally reached the point where, if I were ever going to be able to walk or stand for any length of time again, I had to put my faith in someone else's hands for a while and have yet more metal added to my spine.

My surgeon told me that I would have to basically relearn a few fundamental motor skills in order to resume a normal life. I remember "passing the test" before I was released from the hospital on a cold January morning. I had to climb a flight of stairs with the help of a strong-armed nurse and my loving and compassionate life partner. So with my husband on one side and the nurse on the other, we made that first walk—together.

That was merely the beginning of a very long, painful recovery process. I would relearn how to walk with the aid of a walker and my very persistent two-year-old granddaughter. In order to continue my rehab at home, I was required to walk for five of every twenty minutes while wearing a back brace and often a bone growth stimulator as well. I recall the awkwardness of trying to cope with the simplest of tasks while this extremely cumbersome electronic devise was strapped to my back. However, the surgeon had advised me of its importance in order to grow bone where it no longer existed throughout my spine. I spent the days sitting at the dining room table with an alarm to remind my little walking companion that it was once again time to encourage Grandma to redevelop a skill that she herself had just mastered not long before.

Forever and Always

Once my daughter-in-law and granddaughter returned to their home after a two-week stay with us, my rehabilitation fell into the hands of my loving and capable husband. Andy would be there to take my hand every step of the way, and I grew to lean on him for almost everything. Once I was strong enough to walk outside, he would lace up my tennis shoes for me, and we would venture out into the vast outdoors arm in arm.

The doctors had warned me that any skills I hadn't reclaimed within a year would most likely be lost forever. Before I knew it, a year had passed. I was now doing many things for myself again, but I still had not regained the ability to tie those tennis shoes. At one point, depression set in. While this is not uncommon for individuals dealing with chronic pain, it was still one more hurdle to overcome, and we did together.

Andy continued to be there for me through it all, and we both learned how to adjust and deal with my restrictions. Then suddenly and without warning, I found myself facing life's challenges alone.

Looking back, I recall that feeling of panic and despair. My world had been ripped from me with no advance notice, and I had to learn how to live a new and unwanted life—alone.

I remember so well the first time I tied those tennis shoes for myself after Andy died. It was as if I were an infant taking her first steps without parental assistance. I suspect that was the moment when I realized that, while life was not necessarily going to be easy, I could do this—so I did!

With the love and support of my family and more friends than I ever could have imagined in my life, I've made necessary changes and rebuilt a life I could learn to accept.

I realized that without Andy in my world, I could no longer reside in it either—so I made a new one.

CHAPTER 1

A Widow's Prison

They'd shared a special weekend together just days before. An out-of-state family wedding offered them the opportunity to celebrate once more, arm in arm, dancing to the song they had designated as "theirs" at their own wedding reception nearly twenty-three years prior. The band played, and Melody nestled up comfortably against Mike's chest, feeling his heart beating so strongly, with no idea that it was destined to stop suddenly just two days later.

It was a weekend of wonderful celebration and then a brisk return to reality. Melody returned to her home office by day while Mike headed back out on the road, driving his tractor–trailer each night.

He placed a kiss gently on her cheek as he had done so many nights before. She looked back at him with an affectionate smile as if to say, "Goodnight, my love!" His baby-blue eyes sparkled as he shot her a playful wink. She never imagined that it would be the last time she would see his charming face.

He left the bedroom they had shared for nearly a quarter of a century. As he stood on the front porch, as usual, he dialed her phone number to say one last "Bye for now" as he made his way out to the truck. She closed her eyes with a sense of security and warmth—a feeling she was about to realize she might never know again. Melody slept with worry-free dreams while fate was dealing her an unwelcomed hand.

An abrupt awakening by her youngest son, standing at her bedside at 3:00 a.m. became a moment that would be etched in her mind forever. The sound startled her as she heard the quiet voice saying "Mom, you need to wake up." As Melody sensed his presence, she exited her slumber. She opened her eyes and immediately began to wonder why he had entered her room in the middle of the night, as she saw William standing next to the bed in her downstairs bedroom. "Mom, the police are waiting for you on our front porch. They have advised me to tell you to get dressed and come upstairs immediately. The officers say it's important," he whispered softly and with little emotion.

It was as if someone had stabbed a knife into her heart. Even before her feet hit the floor, she knew in her heart that the world she had grown to know and rely upon was coming to an end. She felt like a prisoner on Death Row, taking that final walk toward the gas chamber. With each step, she felt her breath becoming more labored as her mind began putting up a wall to avoid what was about to befall her.

With trembling hands, Melody slowly turned the knob and stepped out onto the porch where Mike had stood just hours before when he'd placed that final goodnight call to her. The police captain began by asking, "Mrs. Cass, do you know

Michael Cass?" With tears in her eyes, she mumbled a reserved "yes, he's my husband." With that, the police officers asked permission to enter the home. "We think you should sit down as we have something to tell you." She heard so little of the words they spoke, but the message had been received. The news of his death hit her as if she had been a passenger on that deadly ride. Her soul mate had been catastrophically removed from the equation, and she had no idea what to do next. William then glanced into the eyes of his mother and witnessed a look he had never seen before. She had become so withdrawn, as if she were barely conscious to the world around her. The police sargent, realizing that Melody was trembling so much that she was having difficulty standing, and had begun struggling for air, decided to contact paramedics. Within moments they arrived and were eventually able to stabilize her uncontrollable vital signs.

Once she began to regain her composure, she found herself surrounded by family and friends, but she felt alone. It was as if she had been placed in solitary confinement. It was a prison she shared with no one. She was housed there all by herself. It was a widow's prison.

Life would never be the same for her. She knew that a love like hers and Mike's comes along only once in a lifetime. She was now sentenced to walk down the path of life alone, with only memories of brighter days that were long gone.

While she rarely found herself without family and friends by her side for the first several days, she still could only see her dark and lonely existence. She realized that she would never feel Mikes arms around her again, no matter how much she longed for them..

With her children's hands clenching hers, she struggled through the days ahead when she was faced with the task of saying good-bye forever to the one person she needed by her side now more than ever.

That first day or two, she was too busy to see how strong the hold was that grief had upon her. There were plans to make and people to inform. Those days were loaded with "busy work," something that she would soon realize was her saving grace.

Before she knew it, the funeral had begun, and she was surrounded by other mourners, although none of them felt the pain quite as deeply as she did. The minister began talking, and the room filled with what in her mind seemed to be an eerie silence. Melody's mind had wandered, trying its best to avoid the feelings that were attempting to consume her. As he began the service, the minister called out her name. This offered her an opportunity, although ever so briefly, to join the conscious attendees. She listened attentively to his words, drawing comfort whenever possible. Yet she still felt so alone.

Then, as suddenly as people had appeared by her side, they vanished. She awoke on what she soon would refer to as "day fifteen" only to find herself completely alone. It was the first day that no one came to the house or even called. In fact, not even a sympathy card arrived in the mail on that day. She longed for someone to just stop by to make her eat or drink. Normal daily functions had become completely unrealistic for her. Even a trip to the local grocery store was more than she could handle. She felt that her life was now being analyzed by everyone close to her, as if she were living under a microscope. No one could understand the feelings that plagued her every thought, and she had no way of climbing out of this deep abyss that engulfed her now.

For weeks she wrapped herself up in a cocoon of grief, just trying to cope with the chore of breathing, feeling like nothing would ever be simple again. In time, the pain would ease, but life's tasks were now left for her to deal with alone in her widow's prison.

CHAPTER 2

Love in a Stranger's Kitchen

𝓜elody realized that she now had only a lifetime of memories to aid her in coping with this new and unwanted life that she had been handed. She reflected on a simpler time: the day she met the man who turned her world around. For a brief moment, she traveled back in time in her mind, and it forced a smile upon her face—something she hadn't been able to accomplish lately. She recalled the time when she arrived at her friend Anne's home with hope merely for consolation and advice. She had no idea what was about to appear before her eyes.

While they had spent quite a bit of time together during the past year, she had never actually stepped foot inside Anne's parents' home. Once inside, she viewed it as a modest house with a large, country-style kitchen. The two girls sat down at the kitchen table, and Melody began discussing the events of the previous day. She had been dating someone whom she had begun to trust and rely upon. Her discovery of an act of betrayal on his part had left her feeling quite melancholy and alone.

She was feeling a deep aching in her heart. But this was not the first time she'd experienced this type of betrayal, and trust wasn't something she could easily give. Melody hadn't allowed anyone to hold a piece of her heart since once, as a teenager, she had loved deeply and without reservation. That had been her first real encounter with the intensity and stronghold that often comes with young love. That relationship had ended abruptly, leaving her feeling scared and alone.

But as the young love died, Melody had been presented with the news that a new life was about to come forth. She then had the thought only of the impending arrival of a small child to care for alone to occupy her mind, while her high school sweetheart sought comfort in the arms of another. She knew that her life had to advance to the next stage. Melody could no longer think only of herself. The couple had promised to spend their lives together, but Melody came to realize that this was no longer an option. She had to do what was best for her unborn child—even if it caused her heart to shatter.

Now a few years had passed since she had experienced that initial pain. She found herself sitting in her friend's kitchen, aching from those same feelings of loneliness and distrust once again.

Melody had spent the better part of the past two years in the arms of a man who even her young son had begun to trust and admire. Now that was gone too, and she had to find a way to cope not only with the emptiness his absence left behind but also to comfort her three-year-old son. She realized that he too would feel the void as this relationship ended, and that hurt her more than the feelings of her own heartache. More than ever, she felt that trust would never be freely given, or quite possibly earned, by anyone ever again.

When she had arrived at her friend's home, Melody had no idea that her life was about to change—forever! The two young women began thoroughly discussing Melody's situation. The hours passed quickly and daylight was approaching. Melody revealed that she felt it would be foolish for her to ever open her heart to anyone again.

Realizing that daybreak was near, Melody arose to her feet and began preparing to leave for home. She thanked Anne for allowing her to express the deep emotions she had been feeling. She once again stated her stance that it was unlikely she would ever trust again as she headed for the door. But suddenly she realized that as quickly as her heart had begun to close off, a slight ray of hope walked through the kitchen door in the form of a stranger, heading to the oven with a box of cherry turnovers in hand.

Why, in all the time she had spent with her friend during the previous year, had there never been mention of this man? Who was he? Where did he belong? Melody saw something in him that she had never seen in anyone. There was a warmth about him even though it was masked by his quiet demeanor. The sturdy, masculine frame made her see him as a protector, a quality she had never really found in men who previously had been a part of her life. This intrigued her as she had considered past experiences that had left her feeling so vulnerable. No words were actually exchanged between the two individuals on this particular night, but she suddenly felt the need to learn more of his existence.

Then one night, Anne, along with Mike's two sisters, arranged a surprise meeting for them. Though Melody had never been viewed as outspoken, she showed little reluctance in conversing with this man who had recently peaked her curiosity. "Melody, this is my step brother Mike. He is in town waiting for his next long haul. Mike is a truck driver." With that, Anne turned toward Mike to continue the introductions. "Mike, this is my friend Melody. I just felt that you two should meet." This seemed to be the only icebreaker that was needed. "It's a pleasure to meet you," Mike replied with a little hesitation as he spoke with a slight stutter. She realized that he too seemed to be sharing a desire to learn more. They spent several hours that first night just sitting and talking. Within weeks Melody and Mike had discovered a lot about each other. They had become almost inseparable. Much to her surprise, in time he would earn the trust she felt sure that she had become incapable of giving to anyone. Their moments together became less sporadic and were meaningful to them both.

Mike was an extremely patient man, and he learned to accept Melody's inability to freely give the part of herself that her previously failed relationships had taken from her. He initially perceived her as an injured bird, but he knew that his love was strong enough to overcome any obstacle. In time he knew that she would grow to trust him—and she did. As a result of his deep and apparent unconditional love, she had begun to acquire strength unlike anything she ever could have imagined for herself.

Two years after they met, this "kitchen stranger" would place a ring on her finger, and they would begin building a beautiful life together.

That first year as husband and wife, they learned even more about one another, and she found a way to put her trust in him completely. She had fallen so deeply in love with him—a feeling she now realized she had never experienced before. The son she had begun raising just five years before would soon take his last name as well, and a family would be formed.

Joe had longed for a daddy for as long as he could remember. Now this five-year-old boy had realized his dreams too. In time, a judge would declare him to be legally Mike's son, at which time a new and unbreakable bond would form. A couple of years later, Joe not only had a daddy but also a new baby brother when William joined the family.

As it often seems to happen in life when happiness enters the picture, time marched on. Four years later, they purchased the home that would host years of memories, and she grew to find a strong feeling of devotion and love between the brick walls and the family who resided there.

Melody was on top of the world. For what seemed to be the first time in her life, she had it all. Her world felt complete. She had learned to relax and live life watching her children grow, holding the hand of the man she loved more than life itself. She knew that it was the love she had been destined to find. Melody hadn't searched to find this special person. He came into her life just before dawn during that night in April as if that were a cosmic plan intended just for her. She had needed him more than she knew, and he came into her world at the moment when she needed him most. While it wasn't given freely or without reservation at first, Melody did grow to completely trust this late-night stranger who had so unexpectedly walked into her life and stolen her heart. She had found love in a stranger's kitchen.

CHAPTER 3

Watching for Signs

Suddenly Melody found herself back in reality. She would soon discover that these brief "trips" back in time, even if only in her mind, would become the best friends she had now.

During the first several days after Mike's death, eating and sleeping really didn't seem to be an option for Melody. She found herself keeping busy with mundane tasks, hoping that she would eventually drop from exhaustion. It just didn't seem to happen for her now. Grief had injected into her an adrenaline-type drug that just kept her moving at full speed.

Within days after Mike's funeral, his side of the closet had been sorted and belongings distributed. Melody now realized that she had to face the daunting task of approaching his garage. It had been his "man cave." She never stepped foot inside the garage unless it was to approach him for assistance with a honey-do chore or to call him in for dinner. Now it was her responsibility too, and she knew that she had to face it head on. After all, the grass wasn't going to stop growing, and the dogs needed to be fed.

While Melody knew the difference between a phillips screwdriver and its flathead counterpart, that was the extent of her mechanical inclination. How was she going to begin to sort through the mounds of tools scattered around his workbench? With the same diligence she had used in the busy work of the previous days she began the task, approaching it with almost a form of tunnel vision. Melody's fingers touched every item in that garage, one tool at a time. As she looked closer at the one place Mike had kept completely to himself, she discovered something that brought happy tears to her eyes. Tacked up on the pegboard backdrop that stared back at him during the times he worked on his projects there, he had been looking ahead at pictures displayed prominently in the most unlikely places. With a smile now gleaming on her face, she now realized that even when he had worked on his projects outside she was never far from his thoughts. Melody now noticed that Mike had pictures of her everywhere. While her observations didn't make her loneliness any easier to bear, she did realize that life had to go on, even though she just wanted to curl up and succumb to an overwhelming feeling that part of her had died as well.

Melody thought back to a "sign" that presented itself as her children escorted her to his funeral. As they exited the driveway, Joe implemented the rule used by his dad for so many years: the driver controls the radio dials as part of the privilege of driving. With that in mind, he chose a radio station that was familiar to him. Although it was her car, Melody really didn't mind. Her thoughts were so far away from their current place and time.

Within seconds, Journey's "Open Arms" rang joyously from the car speakers. Tears began to form in her eyes as Melody thought back to the night so many years before, when she and Mike had exchanged their vows, held one another close, and danced to this song for the very first time as husband and wife. Realizing that this was not a song Joe had ever heard playing on "his station" in the past, the thought of Mike's presence on this journey overwhelmed the whole family. "Their song" was playing—as if it were a message directly from Melody's beloved—meant just for her. For that split second, the young widow felt less alone than she had felt in days. It was the first sign that told her that even though Mike was no longer in her world, their love lived on. She would find this to be the case periodically—especially when she needed him most.

Now Melody was finding observations unlike any she had ever seen before. She recalled returning from the funeral and walking into the kitchen. She saw something she never would have expected: an illuminated heart had appeared mysteriously on a kitchen cabinet. While the same nightlight had burned along the back wall of the kitchen for several years, it had never created this type of light and there was no logical reason why it should. This was accompanied by a strange silence that consumed the house when a cuckoo clock that had meant so much to her seemed to have stopped ticking at the same moment.

The kitchen seemed to be the one place she now found herself unable to occupy. While it was the one room in the house where Melody had always felt that she excelled, she could no longer even enter it without bursting into tears. Mike had always been her biggest motivation and a true advocate of anything she created in that room. Now with the image on the cabinet it had become unbearable for her to enter.

The heart had been a symbol Mike had used throughout their years together when he wanted to remind her that above all else, his love was true and never ending. She recalled their first wedding anniversary. Mike had presented her with a stuffed animal that appeared to be holding a heart shaped picture frame. Inside the frame was a photograph of the two of them taken at their wedding. In addition, around the animal's neck was a birthstone pendant. This too was in the shape of a heart. That was the first of many such gifts from him. During their years together, Melody had noticed that whenever he couldn't seem to express his love with words he would give her a heart. She had known the depth of Mike's love for her and she now felt that his spirit was standing beside her saying the words "I love you with all of my heart." Ironically, the same things that had once made her feel so loved now made her feel so alone.

For the first several months, just the idea of a new month beginning without Mike in her life was more than she could bear to comprehend. Before she knew it, busy work had become harder to find. Projects that had held Melody's interests while Mike was in her world no longer appealed to her. It was almost as if everything she'd known had been turned inside out. At times, she even felt as though her skin had been ripped away. She felt empty—alone! Melody knew that she had to recreate herself and this new life that had been forced upon her without warning or desire.

Melody once suffered, but had overcome depression, a result of the chronic pain she'd felt due to injuries she had sustained in a car accident several years before. More than ever now, she knew that she had to remain strong. With that in mind, Melody began traveling.

A solo road trip on backcountry roads to a state she'd not seen since she was an infant, to visit her big brother and his family, would teach her the first lessons she needed to rebuild her life. She called to ask if they would welcome a brief visit. Their reply was a resounding yes. So within hours, suitcases were packed and she was on her way.

As she headed out of town, Melody stopped by the local tire store where she was informed that, while her tires weren't in great shape, they would be fine for the trip. However, the tire store employee also advised her to be extremely careful on slick pavement, as the tread was rather badly worn. She took his warning under advisement and headed toward Minnesota. Only miles into Missouri, she found herself driving through a remote area when suddenly rain began to pour down. After hydroplaning numerous times, she found herself praying.

Before she knew it, her thoughts consisted only of her pleading, "Please, dear Lord, either dry this pavement of get me safely to a tire store." No sooner than she reached the crest of the next hill, she spotted a rack of new tires in front of a small mom-and-pop shop. It was at that point when Melody realized something that became fundamental in her grieving process. In fact, before this moment, she had struggled to find the will to live. Now she was hearing her own voice echoing from within. She suddenly discovered that, even though every step she took now was more difficult than she could have ever imagined, and she missed Mike so much, she still wanted to live. The fact that she found herself praying for safety made her see that she still wanted to carry on—she had to carry on! So Melody bought four new tires and continued her journey down the windy backcountry roads through Iowa and into Minnesota.

The sights and sounds struck her in a way that left her with a feeling of awe. Melody had never traveled these roads before, and many of the landmarks along the way amused her. However, it wasn't the buildings or road signs giving her this feeling, but a new perspective that she had gained toward them. At one time she actually caught herself chuckling at the sight of a barn painted black and white in an effort to resemble a cow. Could this be why Mike had loved his job so much? Did he have this same insight? After all, Mike had dealt with great loss early in his life when first his mother died and then again with the tragic loss of his older brother.

She now found herself looking at objects, observing the humor in them. In what seemed like a "first" for her, Melody merely turned on her cruise control, set at the speed limit, and changed the vehicle's direction whenever the navigation system advised her that it was necessary. She had no time constraints or responsibilities. For the first time in her life, she felt the need to just let life live itself for a while.

Although her visit was relatively short at her brother's house, Melody began feeling a sense of healing. She found a way to laugh among her tears. She spent time sitting and just sharing memories of the happy times, realizing all she had now were memories of moments with Mike and knowing that no more could ever be created.

During dinner at a Hibachi grill, Melody noticed yet another sign. After distributing rice to everyone else seated around the grill, the chef formed her rice into the shape of a heart. As though he was seeing deep into her soul, feeling what she was feeling, he gently placed the spatula beneath the mound of heart-shaped rice. With a precise and gentle movement, he lifted the shaped food, making it appear as though it were beating, and then looked directly at her and said, "This heart is for you!" How could he have possibly known just how important a mere shape had become to her, let alone how badly she needed to see it?

While there were so many signs that presented themselves during those initial months, the one that still remained lit for months after his death was the heart that appeared on her kitchen cabinet in their family home. She had grown to rely on that simple shape that continued to remind her of his love every time she saw it. This heart seemed to pull her back home, to a place she otherwise would have avoided—possibly forever. The experience of this first trip taught Melody that she had a way to at least briefly escape the pain when it seemed to overwhelm her.

Another month passed and Melody decided to take another trip, this time to visit some dear friends that she and

Mike had often spoken of visiting over the years, although they had never actually gone. She boarded a plane heading to Phoenix. During this visit, she began giving thought to what direction her life should take. Phone conversations with Joe and William caused her to think about decisions involving the large family home back in Illinois. She remembered the burdens that came along with maintaining that home—now by herself.

While William was attending the university in town near their home, Joe, Christine, and Brooke were temporarily living in Indiana, as Joe was completing his military training. The boys expressed feelings that it might be a good idea for Melody to be close to Joe and his family while they awaited the arrival of their next child. "Mom, William and I think you should get an apartment in Indiana for a few months while I finish training. Then Christine and I will find a home that is big enough for us all when I find out where I am to be stationed next. You can stay with us for a few years until you feel ready to find a home that you can call your own," stated Joe. This offer meant so much to Melody.

This was not a choice that she found easy to make. Any way she looked at it, she would be separated from at least one of her children in a time when she just needed her family close to her.

Once again, she looked to the heavens and prayed for guidance. She realized that as long as that heart illuminated her kitchen cabinet, she could never leave their family home. But that seemed to be all that held her there now. William was old enough, and she knew that he needed the opportunity to make his own way in the world. Melody feared that he would never feel free to try as long as they shared a roof.

Her time with friends in Arizona seemed also to play a part in teaching her how to cope in this new world. Melody had discovered that taking breaks from her everyday life seemed almost life saving for her at times. Mike was never out of her thoughts, neither did she expect that he ever would be. But distractions for her became almost a way of making existence easier to bear.

The Arizona visit had been nice, but Melody realized that she had to return home. At this point, she had begun to observe a pattern. Spontaneity seemed to be an attribute she now possessed. As quickly as she had made the decision to take the trip, she now had formed the conclusion that it was time to return. Once home, she was startled to find that the decision that had been so difficult for her to make had actually been made easier. The heart had removed itself from the kitchen cabinet as mysteriously as it had appeared just two months earlier.

Not long after that, she made arrangements to sell the family home and move into a small, one-bedroom apartment a mile away from her oldest son and his family. It seemed to work out well for everyone. Melody now was close enough to spend time with her granddaughter, who she missed so very much, and William was given the opportunity to rent his bedroom from the new owners of the house he'd called home for years.

Melody had little doubt that this was the right decision. After all, she didn't feel as though she had made it alone. She had been watching for signs.

CHAPTER 4

"Daddy"

Melody had now turned two pages on the calendar since the horrific night when the police had come knocking on her front door. Although she had begun sleeping more than just a few minutes here and there, she was still wondering if normal sleep would ever return for her. Her grief had become so strong that it blocked any hope of dreams when she slumbered. She knew that dreams were her only chance to spend time with the love of her life. This had become clear to her one night after she had collapsed from total exhaustion. She silently and unexpectedly closed her eyes for a brief moment, and before she realized that any time had passed, her eyes reopened. Melody awoke to discover that she had dreamed of Mike. This wasn't like any dream she had ever experienced before. It had left her feeling that she had actually been spending that time with him. During this dream, a few questions were answered and some assurances were made. At one point during her dream, she actually felt his lips pressing on hers and even thought she had smelled his cologne.

Since Mike had been taken from her so suddenly, they had never discussed his feelings about subjects that a married couple approaching a predicted end might work through. This had left Melody feeling unsure of how he would feel about such matters as making life decisions and other desires for her in the event of his death. The message that became abundantly clear to her in this dream, above all else, was his wish for her happiness. He wanted her to find peace in a world where he no longer could reside.

Melody also discovered as she opened her eyes that she had lain in an unfamiliar position during her slumber. She had slept with her arms wrapped around her body as if she had been giving herself a hug. She recalled feeling as though Mike's arms had been embracing her during her dream. Melody began to understand that Mike was consoling her in the best way he could now. This caused her to develop a sense of strength and determination, something she had lacked up to this point. Although it wasn't the way she had wanted her life to be, Melody was beginning to see that she could, in time, survive this terrible ordeal that had consumed her life now that Mike was no longer by her side. She seemed to awaken with a new sense of peace.

However, as much as Melody longed for just a few stolen moments with him now, dreams didn't become a common practice for her just yet. Since dreams weren't happening, daydreams were her only refuge.

She thought back to the early days of her life together with Mike—back when Joe was merely a toddler. She recalled the day when the four-year-old child had accepted Mike fully into his life. His friends all had a male role model who resided full time in their lives, and he wanted one too. Melody recalled one particular day when Joe returned home from preschool and was greeted by this man who had become a permanent fixture in their lives. He had been spending much of his time with them for a year or so now. With no forethought or warning, the small boy innocently blurted out the word "Dad" in reference to Mike as if he'd been using that term for years.

While Melody could see that it flattered Mike, she also witnessed something else in him in response to Joe's declaration. Mike almost immediately sat down in a chair nearby and then called out to Joe. The small boy climbed upon his lap while Mike proceeded to tell him, "You know I care about you very deeply and hope that someday I can call you 'son.' But right now I am your friend." With that, he released the small child, took Melody into his arms, and with a slight tear in his eye, he explained his stance. "You know that I love both you and Joe with all of my heart. That is why I've asked him not to call me 'Daddy' yet. While I see us building a life together, we have made no commitments to one another. I feel that his pain would be much deeper if we didn't stay together after allowing him to think of me that way."

Melody knew in her heart that Mike was right, and she hoped that Joe would understand too. Mike stated that it would be much more painful for the boy to lose a dad than it would be just to lose a friend if the relationship didn't work out. Melody saw the wisdom in his thoughts. She realized that he wasn't out to gain popularity or win her over. He had placed the best interests of Melody and even more so, that of her young child, above his own. This hadn't been a common occurrence in her life. The truth of the matter was that if she had to put her finger upon a date on the calendar when she had discovered herself completely in love with this man, this would have been the day. For the first time in years, Melody had found something that had been missing in her heart. She realized that she could actually trust Mike.

As for Joe calling Mike "Daddy," that word was not mentioned again until six months later when Mike placed a simple ring upon Melody's finger and said, "I do," while gazing into her eyes. After dancing their first dance as husband and wife, Mike swept Joe, now five years old, into his arms and said, "Now you can call me 'Daddy.'"

From that day forward, Joe never called Mike anything else. One day it would be official, but for now it was enough for him in name only. With the biggest smile etched on his face for what seemed like forever, this little boy was happier than he could have ever imagined. He now had a daddy.

CHAPTER 5

Another Reason to Smile

Melody suddenly leapt back into reality and realized that their next grandchild would never get the opportunity to meet the grandfather who had longed for her arrival.

She recalled how, just months before, during a phone call on Mother's Day, another reason to smile was placed upon Mike's face. Joe had called to inform his parents that he and his wife were expecting another child.

Melody had never met a man who adored children as much as Mike had. She recalled that he had told her early on in their relationship that he wanted eight kids—he loved children! Melody was able to give him the two boys, but a health condition prevented her from having more children. Mike never spoke of his wish for a larger family again. It no longer seemed to matter to him. He loved his family and never made Melody think that his life was anything less than complete.

Her mind drifted back once again to just a few short years before his death. She remembered the huge smile that had appeared upon his face the day their first little granddaughter, Brooke, was born. Melody loved seeing that look on his face and realized how much she wished that she could have blessed him with the large family he had wanted all those years ago. But she knew in her heart that he cherished his family just the way it was.

Hearing the news that another grandchild would be joining the family soon, she was thrilled that her son was able to give him yet another child to love. Mike longed for this new arrival and spoke of his joy often.

After Mike's death, the fact that he would now never get to meet his second grandchild plagued Melody. She felt an obligation to make this child realize that Grandpa was admiring her from the heavens above.

When her grief had subsided somewhat, she once again experienced a dream. This time Mike informed her that she would be meeting their second granddaughter soon and that he was holding her tightly until the time when she could put her arms around the newborn child. It was shortly after this dream that Melody sold the family home, packed her belongings into a truck with the aid of several friends, and began the next phase of her life—living alone. This was something she had not done before. There would be no children and no husband to care for now. She had to learn how to create her own world.

Melody hopped into her car with her dogs resting comfortably in the passenger seat. Several friends followed behind in a large van that contained her most important material possessions. She had known that downsizing from a 2,600-square-foot home into a small space would be a feat. But most material possessions seemed to hold little value to her now. She still felt such deep loss—a hole in her heart that no mere object could fill.

Getting settled into her five-hundred-square-foot apartment seemed to be the easy part—starting a new life wasn't quite so simple. Melody was so thankful to have Joe and his family nearby, but it was quite an adjustment for her in this big city.

Her dogs seemed to feel the stress of the new situation every bit as much as she did, but they adapted in the best way they could. They had had an acre of land at their former home, and adjusting to the twenty feet of grass designated as a "pet area" wasn't easy for them. Melody knew that she was going to have to find a way to comfort their pain if she ever had hopes of rebuilding a normal life. Due to new behavioral issues, she never felt comfortable leaving them unattended for more than a few minutes at a time. After months of hardly leaving her apartment, she hired a trainer who came by to teach them how to live in their new environment. Her efforts did make the situation more bearable, but it didn't give them complete resolution. But the hardest part for Melody was witnessing the pain when she looked into their eyes.

Melody learned a new routine very quickly and even joined a musical group to give her a reason to leave home once in a while. Shopping with Joe's wife, Christine, and little Brooke became routine and gave her something to look forward to every week. She made it her mission to keep her pregnant daughter-in-law walking whenever she could.

Shortly before the arrival of the newest family member, Joe and Christine came to Melody with news that caused her heart to feel a warmth that it hadn't felt in quite a while. They wanted her to be the first to know that they intended to name their child after Mike. With tears in her eyes, Melody welcomed the news. However, knowing that the newest family member would be named in honor of her late grandfather caused conflicting emotions for Melody. On one hand, she loved the idea that her son wanted to honor his dad's memory this way, but on the other hand, she knew that she would think of him every time anyone called out her name. With the wound that his death had left behind, she wasn't sure if this would be bearable for her. But it didn't take long for her to realize that the honor she felt on Mike's behalf would far outweigh the pain.

Just five short months after saying good-bye to Mike, Melody said hello to Mika. While she was a relatively quiet and calm baby, Mika seemed to be extra warm with her grandma. If ever there was a smile that could melt her heart, it was the beaming twinkle Melody saw in this newborn's eyes. In her heart, Melody knew that Mike had already wrapped his loving arms around this child, but she now was so happy when the world got to finally welcome little Mika. She realized that this new family member had given Melody another reason to smile.

CHAPTER 6

Sharing Parenthood

The newborn child looked so much like her daddy from day one. Melody thought back to when her own children were young. Joe and William had been her purpose for so many years, along with Mike, of course. Her life with them had been more than she ever dreamed it could be. She'd had her three guys in her life, and they were the center of her universe. She continued to look back to days long gone.

As far as Joe was concerned, Mike had always been his dad; he had never really acknowledged anyone else as such. At the time of the adoption, Joe was seven years old. The family was also just a few short months away from welcoming another baby into their world.

They were expecting William, and Melody had given Mike the task of deciding whether or not to unveil the gender of their new bundle of joy prior to the actual arrival. He decided to leave the question unanswered until the child was born. She had her misgivings about leaving such questions unanswered, but Melody had made the choice to learn Joe's gender before his birth years before. Since Mike had not been in her life yet at that point, he'd had no say in the matter. Melody felt that it was only fair to leave the decision to Mike this time.

Six weeks passed, and while the calendar indicated that they still had several weeks to wait, William began to show signs of impatience. He decided to make his debut nearly seven weeks early. Instead of a cool October day, he arrived on a hot, steamy Sunday in late August.

Melody remembered the day so vividly. She hadn't been feeling well for a week or longer, but the doctor assured her at an appointment just two days earlier that all was well. She had gone to bed early on that Saturday evening, realizing that the following day was going to be busy. There was to be a reunion on Sunday afternoon, and she had family members in town for the occasion. The day was to kick off with a golf game for Mike with several of his in-laws. Then it would be lunch at the park in a neighboring town with several people Melody had been longing to see.

The reunion took place as planned, but Mike and Melody did not attend. William had other plans for them that day, and although she had informed Mike of her suspicions that his child was not going to wait much longer, she agreed that he should move forward with the morning golf game as planned.

Melody's family members arrived at their house to accompany Mike to the golf course at around eight o'clock that morning. However, within the hour, family members who had stayed behind were making a mad dash to locate Mike out on the golf course. As Melody was being escorted to her mother's car, Mike came driving up the alley to their house. Had it not been for an intrusive and persistent telemarketer as she was walking out the door, Melody would have surely been well on her way to the hospital by the time he had arrived home.

At 11:54 a.m. on that steamy August morning, the family welcomed William into their world. Considering the fact that he had arrived into the world ahead of schedule, he seemed to be very healthy. However, a phone call from the doctor's office with test results just a few days after they had brought their little boy home, caused Mike and Melody to immediately return William to the hospital. They discovered that he had an underdeveloped liver and there was concern of potential brain damage due to a severe case of jaundice. This gave Melody the opportunity to witness firsthand just how truly loyal Mike was toward his young family. Upon William's hospital admission, Mike called upon close family members to watch over Joe. Once their firstborn was safely and temporarily housed with other family members, Mike returned to the hospital and instructed the nurses that he would be in need of a cot. He refused to leave the room during that hospital stay except to make a daily visit to spend time with Joe. Otherwise Mike stayed by Melody's side and together they struggled with the sight of their suffering child.

As soon as the doctors felt safe in releasing him, Mike and Melody brought William home once again, and they spent the years ahead watching their children grow into wonderful young men. Melody felt that she had the world at her fingertips. Her life was more complete than she ever had imagined it would be. She loved spending her life with Mike and the boys—sharing parenthood.

CHAPTER 7

Without Him

As a young widow, Melody had realized early in her grieving process that she was going to have to find a way to get herself through the days and years that lay ahead. She recalled the years when she had spent so much of her time and energy on her husband and sons that she hadn't been nurturing many deep friendships. She'd maintained limited relationships with a few people from her former single years, but for the most part, she had been playing the wife and mother roles almost exclusively.

She was surprised to find so many people not only welcoming her back into their lives after so many years but actually reaching out to her and wanting to make her a part of their lives after Mike's accident. While she valued these friendships and welcomed the love and support they offered, Melody also found herself pulling away from those who seemed to offer too much guidance. She realized that it was going to take her own inner strength to pull through, and she was terrified that she would allow herself to lean on anyone too much if given the opportunity.

This had been only a small part of the factors that had made her feel the need to leave the home that she and Mike had shared with their family. She felt that at times it was as though some of these outreached arms were just drama seekers. As with any unexplained death, the facts and details of the accident were never made clear to anyone. This was a difficult realization for Melody. She wanted answers, but there seemed to be none. Melody tried to keep her mind from spending much time analyzing the details, but the questions seemed to follow her no matter where she went. While she had been told facts about the crash, there were still many details left undiscovered. It had been quite catastrophic, and the details of what they did know of how he died had been very hard for her to think about, much less discuss with anyone. It seemed to her as though people were trying to place blame for what appeared to be nothing more than a freak accident. She just couldn't bear the fact that wherever she went, questions ensued. He was a professional driver who took his job quite seriously. She was finding it difficult to accept that people seemed to want to know what he had done wrong.

The most frequently asked questions were "Did he have a heart attack?", or "Did he fall asleep?" The autopsy revealed no health reasons, and with the knowledge that he had only left the trucking terminal two hours prior, that was unlikely as well. Since the other party involved in the accident had moved from the original crash site, no investigation was ever performed. Melody had to accept that answers may never be found. She wanted everyone else to realize that too. Instead it appeared to her as if people thought she was hiding something. That just wasn't the case. They weren't going to get an inside story from her because she too had more questions than answers. There was nothing to hide—she had just been left to find her way alone through her despair.

There were times when a simple trip to the grocery store often left her feeling angry and cold. Simply waiting in a checkout line was too much human interaction for her. She soon realized that there was nowhere safe to hide from the impact of reality slapping her in the face. She began stalling to take her necessary trips, going to twenty-four-hour stores in the middle of the night whenever possible, waiting until she felt that anyone who might recognize her would most certainly be asleep. She just didn't think she could cope with people who seemed like strangers to her, approaching her from all directions, seeking to find answers to the same questions she found herself asking.

At the same time, placing a movie into the DVD player had a way of invoking a bout of tears that surely would flood the neighborhood if she would just open the front door. Mike had been attempting to watch a movie that Melody had given him for Father's Day, but he hadn't finished viewing it yet. Suddenly the realization that Mike had unfinished tasks and desires seemed to overwhelm her. Everywhere she looked now, Melody saw reminders of him and the life they'd shared.

She knew that she had to find her own way in this world now, and she was not willing to let anyone dictate too much of life's decisions to her. She knew her friends were only trying to offer advice they felt was helpful. But she was aware that she had to follow her own heart. However, at times this was quite difficult. Many friends had tried to encourage her to hold off any decision making during that first year of her grieving, while family members could see how intense the pain was for her. It wasn't an easy path that she now had chosen to follow. How could she explain the need to go against her friends' wishes for her? But Melody had known what she needed to do when she decided to sell the family home just two months after Mike's accident. If she was ever sure of anything, it was that she could no longer reside in the home they had shared together.

Melody thought about those few short months leading up to her leaving town. She didn't want to completely shut people out of her life, but at the same time she felt the need for distance from daily reminders. In her mind, her sanity had come into question. The details of Mike's accident were unimaginably devastating and had left her feeling so cold and alone. It was as if the world was now resting heavily upon her shoulders. Occasionally she bore so much emotional weight that she found it difficult just to breathe. Panic and fear had become such frequent feelings, and she wondered if she would be capable of feeling complete joy ever again.

Melody once again found a pattern forming in her life. She had begun to feel like she was reliving the same emotions. Just when she would feel that she had gotten a grip on one aspect of grief, an event would happen that seemed to suck her right back to the beginning. Melody discovered that grief is a circle. She had to learn to always be prepared for that one moment when something would hit her out of the blue and make her stand up and take notice of her new life and the one she left behind (or that, more correctly stated, had left her behind).

But whenever the reality of life seemed to bring her down the most, signs appeared from out of nowhere to brighten her day. Melody began to feel that it was Mike speaking to her—heart to heart. His spirit seemed to be reminding her of how hard they had fought together to get her through the bout with depression years before as she struggled with the aftermath of chronic pain initially after her automobile accident. Thoughts plagued her as she remembered the struggle and how she had leaned upon him for so much of the strength it had taken to overcome this condition. They had kept much of this between the two of them. Mike had known that their love was strong and that they would be able to overcome almost anything. Now Melody knew that she would have to find a way to get through the tough moments ahead with only the memory of his love and support with her. Melody began using a "fifteen-minute rule."

Whenever she felt a wave of despair or fear taking a grip on her life, she set her kitchen timer for fifteen minutes. Once the timer was set, she would fully allow whatever negative emotions she was encountering to take hold of her. But as soon as the timer would sound, no matter how she was feeling, she had to redirect her thoughts to something constructive.

This distraction soon turned into a blog that was shared and admired by many. Melody found comfort in knowing that her words were helping others who were struggling with grief as well. It often made her realize that she was not as alone in her grief journey as she had initially felt.

Sometimes she concluded a post with a note to Mike, or even wrote the complete blog post as if she were writing it directly to him. Whatever mood struck, Melody let it pour out of her fingertips and onto the keys. During the first few months following his death she posted daily, often numerous times each day. In time, Melody found other ways to channel her emotions and loneliness. But for now, it was with her writing. Since it was a form of therapy for her, she would sit for hours and just "free write." Grammar and spelling never became a concern. She wrote until her heart had finished saying what it had longed to say.

Three weeks after his passing, Melody wrote a blog titled "New Normal? What's Normal." It read like this:

"I want you back in my life… every moment of every day" is the thought that races through my mind as I glance at the picture of you here at my side!

I am told that I have to find my "new normal" now… I don't want to leave my "old normal"… it was safe… comfortable… warm. You taught me things about life and love that I had only heard about before I met you! Now all I have are the memories of you and me… nothing tangible to hold onto anymore!

They told me you were gone… I really didn't believe them for a while. Even after the flowers had all wilted, I still didn't believe it was true. Too much time has passed now… you would be back by my side if you could – I keep reminding myself. The "why's" and "how's" are still so prevalent… encompassing my every thought and mood! How long will I have to carry this burden? I am too young to have to feel this way... too much life ahead of me... too much time to be alone! Yet I can't see my life any other way now!

I look back and wonder why I ever cared about anything else when I so clearly had it all... you were my all... and together we turned it into even more. Our relationship had a dynamic all its own... and we loved that about each other. We had reached a comfortable stage that very few can relate to... and we wouldn't have traded that for anything in the world! Now all I have is the uncomfortable feeling of trying to exist without you!

Everywhere I turn there is a reminder of our last days together... I turn on the DVD palyer to find "Sherlock Holmes"... a movie I bought for you for Father's Day just a couple of months ago. You had started watching the movie weeks before, but something would come up every time... you never saw the end, I'm sure! Maybe someday I will watch it for you... just not yet... it's still too soon!

I keep reminding myself that it is better to have loved and lost than never to have loved at all... still little consolation! I am greedy... I wanted you by my side forever... that is what you promised... that is what I grew to expect.

Now I just hope you are at peace. I feel you with me, and on rare occasion I see you in my dreams... but that is still not enough! Why did you leave me so soon? That question just keeps coming back to me over and over like a broken record. Where did our "forever" go?

I carry you, imbedded in my heart, every moment of every day!

I'll find my "new normal"... someday... somehow. In the meantime, I am so thankful that I had you in my "old normal." I love you Mike... yesterday... today... always!

There were many other blog posts, ranging in topics, but always dealing with Melody's emotions. While the feelings varied, the subject did not. She wrote of her journey down grief's pathway. Although she often wondered why, this raw emotion that poured from her fingertips was often viewed as inspirational. She quickly realized that her fifteen-minute rule was an early source of strength for her, especially when she felt that she had no more inner strength to give.

It seemed ironic to her that comfort would be found by stroking her fingertips upon the computer keyboard. Writing had been Mike's dream for her, not her own. Why was this suddenly such a source of strength for her? Had he been subconsciously preparing her for a life she was destined to live—without him?

CHAPTER 8

"Home"

Melody grew to rely upon her children and found joy in the times she spent with them. They had become closer than she could have ever anticipated while living in Indiana over the eight months since Mike's death. Joe and his family had, in some ways, begun to fill the void she was feeling, as denial continued to fade and bargaining was in full force. There were so many wonderful things happening in her children's lives now, and while she wanted to be a part of it all, it also caused a lot of pain for her. It wasn't difficult for Melody to figure out why, but it was not so easy for her to remedy.

Mike had been in the US Navy as a young adult and was so proud when Joe chose to enlist in the military right out of high school. Now Joe was exceeding his wildest dreams by making a career as an officer in the US Army, after serving many years as an enlisted man. Melody too was proud of the men their boys had become, and she recalled how Mike had beamed with pride when he realized what his influence had done for them. Joe's commissioning ceremony would take place, but Mike would not be in this world to witness it. Meanwhile, William was finishing up the current semester at the university in their hometown. He had decided to move upstate afterward for a better opportunity to pursue his major. Mike and Melody had always seen that he had great potential, but she realized that it would be only for her eyes to see now as William chased his dreams.

While her children's lives were moving forward and following their intended paths, Melody realized that she needed to redirect hers. She was desperately trying to get a grasp on widowhood, and she had felt relieved to have a life near Joe's family to look forward to that included being needed as well as not having to spend her days and nights completely alone. But she wasn't all alone. She had Angel and Hogan, her canine companions, who seemed to be dealing with a form of mourning as well. Melody could see the pain in Angel's eyes, and it was more than she could bear at times. It was a sadness that never seemed to be eased.

She realized that, while the offer she had accepted with Joe and his family was good for her, she had to take her four-legged babies' needs into consideration as well. She had begun to realize that life wasn't about always taking the easy way out. Melody knew that she had to follow her heart even if it caused it to ache more at times.

Even though she had begun to create a life in Indiana, Melody had known that it was only temporary when she moved there. It was never intended as—neither would it ever be—a permanent home for her. However, during her months residing there, Melody had found a church where she felt a sense of belonging. While her loyalty and membership continued at the church she had attended as a child, her physical attendance just wasn't an option now. However, her new temporary church family did make her feel somewhat safe. They knew that she was a widow, but the congregation didn't know anything about Mike. Sometimes that felt like a blessing, but she also missed being able to talk about him with people who could share memories of him with her.

Melody recalled spending time with family and friends before leaving their family home and moving into her apartment. She once more began longing for social interaction. But she knew that moving back to their hometown was a challenge that she just wasn't ready to accept. Visiting was difficult enough for her—living there just wasn't an option that she felt she could even consider.

Joe's time in Indiana was drawing near its end, and Melody felt torn. She knew it would be time to move on one way or another. Although Melody had been eager to follow the plan that had been put into place when she first sold her family home, she was beginning to question her decision. Joe and his family had known that they would be moving within months. That's the way it is when you are in the military, but with his upcoming change in status they knew it was more than just a possibility. She realized that they would be moving at least twice in the upcoming months ahead. It was clear that with Joe's training nearing completion, and his commissioning ceremony approaching, relocation was eminent. Melody had been thrilled when they asked her to move with them and be a part of their everyday lives while her grandchildren were young, but she had now begun to realize that this situation had the potential for her to become dependent upon them. Dependency was not something Melody wanted for herself at this stage of her life. She had been so dependent upon Mike when he was alive. Melody knew that she had to resist the temptation—knowing she could never survive that kind of pain again. The middle-aged widow knew this was not going to be easy for her, but she needed to find a way to discover a life of her own now.

With this contemplation in mind, one evening while Joe was visiting Melody at her humble little one-bedroom apartment, she discussed with him her concerns of their impending plan. He made it clear to her that he felt it was her life as well as her decision. He would support whatever she decided to do. With everything he had accomplished in his twenty-eight years, she couldn't have been more proud of him than she was at that moment. He had become so much like his dad. Although her decision was going to affect the life of his family directly, he refused to try to sway her in any way. It was her choice to make, and he knew she would follow his heart, not hers, if he gave her the chance.

Melody began searching the Internet in an effort to find a place she could accept as home for her and the two canine children she had been left to care for alone. Melody recalled how Angel had been Mike's girl from the moment he spotted her in the pet shop window. Hogan had come along two years later when the couple decided that Angel should produce offspring. It had been a complicated and expensive process, but Hogan was the only result of this attempt. They welcomed him into the family with open arms, but he carried with him the attitude of an overly protected, spoiled child.

Melody's search began with a stroke of the keys in an attempt to find a place she and her dogs could now at least call home for a while. Her criterion was not to be too close to the town where she and Mike, as well as their children, had called home for all of those years but close enough that she could see family and friends from time to time. She mentally pinned a fifty-mile radius on her virtual map and the search began. Several homes appeared to be options for her during her initial search. But the search narrowed when she discovered a home located in a quaint little town that she and Mike used to admire in previous years on their weekend trips to a cabin they had owned along the Mississippi River.

It was not practical for Melody to travel back to inspect the properties that appealed to her. Since they still lived in their old hometown, Melody contacted her parents to ask for assistance in her search.

Meanwhile, she researched the site as well as the foreclosure process, along with the pros and cons involved. It appeared to her that the past experience she'd had as a realtor when her children were small could give her a slight advantage. After chosen options were explored by Melody's parents, and she considered their evaluations of each piece of property, she decided to trust fate and place a bid through an online auction house for a home in foreclosure in this small village in the country. She placed an opening bid and watched as it was soon outbid. Due to the fact that this house had been unseen with the exception of her parents' outdoor inspection, she had a limited budget in mind. She had felt confident that as long as the foundation was solid and the price was right, she could fix anything else that came along. But once she had discovered that she had been outbid, in her heart, she felt that she had to let it go. A sense of disappointment came over her, knowing that this house that had somehow drawn her in would not be an option for her. So with that in mind, her search continued.

The other homes she had discovered during her online search paled in comparison, and actually didn't even exist in one instance. She felt once again a deep sense of loss.

But just hours after the close of the online auction for the home that she had desired, she received a call on her cell phone from an unknown number. Something compelled her to answer this call, and she was surprised when the voice on the other end of the line introduced himself as a representative from the auction house. He was informing her that the other bidder was not able to obtain financing and if she chose to pursue this home, her bid would be considered.

She viewed this as a form of divine intervention. It was as if this house was meant to be hers. While it wasn't a "done deal" since the bank that had held the mortgage on this foreclosed piece of property would have the opportunity to reject her offer, a waiting game began. Melody started packing up belongings that she felt could be done without over the months ahead in hopes of approval from the bank.

She knew that she would be moving somewhere regardless, and she felt somewhat optimistic since the auction house had contacted her about reinstating the bid. She realized that if her bid hadn't at least been worth considering, they never would have called her that day.

Melody kept herself very busy, trying to pass the time without giving the house much thought. But a few weeks went by and still no word. She became very impatient, but what could she do? It was out of her hands, and she knew that she had to accept whatever was to come now. Although it was the last thing she really wanted, Melody was beginning to settle in to the fact that she may have to remain in this one bedroom apartment until something else came along. She considered the possibility that fate was still leading her toward accepting the offer that her kids had presented. Melody knew it would still be a good life for her.

After what seemed like the longest three weeks of Melody's life, an e-mail appeared in her inbox with a contract to purchase. She found herself crying tears of joy. It would mean moving to a strange town where she knew absolutely no one, leaving Joe and his family to move forward in life without her in tow, but she held tightly to her convictions. She had no doubt that she needed to give her children the opportunity to spread their wings and fly—something she feared would not be easy if she became too dependent on them.

Melody knew how hard life could be when she allowed people to get too close now. She had relied on Mike for everything; he was her world. She feared that her heart would never survive another disappointment like the one she felt when she lost him. This was not something she wanted to encounter ever again. With that in mind, she too had to "stick to her guns" with her decision to pursue a life for herself.

One week after the paperwork was completed, Melody packed a few bare necessities into her car and headed back to her hometown to sign papers and then pick up keys to the first home she would ever own entirely by herself. She felt much apprehension and just prayed that Mike would send her a sign, letting her know he approved. No such sign appeared, but Melody forged ahead anyway.

The check was written and the forms were signed, and Melody realized she was now the proud owner of her new home in the country. Having been raised as a Midwest farmer's daughter, moving back to the country was giving her a strong feeling of comfort. She had already found a sense of belonging, just knowing where she was now going to live. But as she left the title company's office, her heart discovered yet another sign to reinforce her feelings. No sooner than she had turned on the ignition in her car, "Open Arms" began to ring out through the car speakers, telling her once more that she had not been alone in this journey.

After a brief stop at the realtor's office, with keys in hand, Melody once more climbed into the driver's seat of the vehicle she'd once shared with the love of her life, continuing on with her journey to view her new purchase firsthand. It was at this point that her gut feeling became more reinforced than she could have ever imagined. With the turning of the key, the radio again began playing "Open Arms"—not once, but twice more!

Just then, as she steered onto the scenic river road that would now be her everyday route to the place she had to learn to call home, she glanced overhead through her car's sunroof to spot an eagle soaring above. This eagle seemed to follow her along this eleven-mile roadway, escorting her home.

Her mind began to wander once more as she recalled how much Mike had loved and admired eagles. For so many years before, Melody and Mike frequented their cabin along the river during "eagle season" in hopes of catching a glimpse of them in flight. This respected bird had even been Mike's profile picture on social media sites.

It became clear to her at this point that her suspicion of divine intervention had been much more than a possibility. She realized that, while he had left it up to her to follow her heart in this decision, Mike wanted her to know that he approved— she was not alone.

She parked the car in the driveway of her new home, and what seemed to be an immediate sense of peace came over her. This feeling hadn't been a part of her emotional makeup for quite some time, but it was a welcomed change.

However, Melody became filled with anticipation as her outreached hand began slowly turning the knob on the front door. She had little idea of what to expect as she had only seen a limited amount of photos prior to the day. As the door opened, joy filled her heart. The bi-level structure was exactly what she had desired. Her biggest fears of home ownership now had miraculously vanished when she realized that the feeling of being overwhelmed, that very same feeling that caused her to leave their family home, no longer existed where she now stood. While the house needed appliances and did require some work, it was clearly livable. Truth be told, it was everything she hoped it would be and more.

Knowing that movers would arrive at her Indiana apartment one week later, Melody got busy trying to decide how to make the most of her new home. As she awaited the arrival of her belongings, Melody intended to make a bed for the dogs as well as herself out of a sleeping bag and a few blankets. But within an hour of her arrival, she began to see how amazing the potential for her new life would be. A neighbor knocked at her door and offered to bring over a spare twin mattress or two for her to use. He had seen that she only had a few belongings with her and realized that he could offer her comfort during the days ahead. She suddenly realized that this was truly the place she belonged. In time she would learn to call this place "home."

CHAPTER 9

Living Life to Its Fullest

Even though she had survived that first year of grieving, Melody still occasionally found herself putting up walls and shutting out those who wanted to help her cope with her new life without Mike. It would have been so easy for her to allow them to ease her pain, but she knew this was her world to conquer now, and she had to forge through and find herself.

She realized that Mike had always lived life with zest while she seemed to spend much of her time watching. Knowing how much she loved standing by his side, Melody struggled with trying to find her identity in the world now. While she didn't want to lose those close to her, she had to stand on her own two feet if she had any hopes of staying strong.

She thought back and realized how far she had come since the days of single life before she had met Mike. Feelings that had once controlled her as a young woman now no longer existed for her, and she was determined to keep it that way. She remembered the strength and wisdom she had acquired through her years with him. Through the losses he had encountered earlier in life, Mike seemed to know how to make the most of whatever was around him. However, this concept didn't always come easy for Melody.

She had grown up learning to fear life. She analyzed her previous years and soon remembered when that fear had first begun. It had happened long before she met Mike, but the fears were so engrained in her that they had become a big part of who she was. That particular day had begun with joy and laughter, and a new adventure was awaiting her. It was her sixteenth birthday, and Melody had never been on a float trip before. With her parents and siblings, as well as many other family members and friends by her side, she anxiously approached the experience. Although she had a slight fear of water, it was far from crippling, so she hopped into the inner tube that awaited her.

Several hours into the float, a tree stuck in the rapidly flowing river would teach Melody a lesson that her teenage self wasn't quite comfortable with learning. She had been pulled toward the obstruction, and it caused her tube to flip, dumping her out. Before she could even realize what had happened, her hands were using every bit of strength possible to grasp the tree, as something more powerful than she could have ever imagined was pulling her down and attempting to take her life. An undertow had a strong grasp on her, and she struggled for what seemed to be a lifetime.

Decades later, she could still recall the thoughts rushing through her mind as she witnessed water rushing viciously overhead. She saw death as eminent and realized that unless a miracle would occur, she would never get her driver's license.

Now as an adult, she could see how silly that thought was, but it was a primary concern to her as a sixteen-year-old girl.

The truth was, she hadn't a lot of experiences to reflect back upon during what she felt were her final moments. Until then, she had thought that she had a lot of years ahead of her. She was suddenly seeing life differently. But in the next moment she felt something trying to pry her locked fingertips from the branch, trying to get her to loosen her grip. Unsure of what was happening, she struggled to keep her hold but finally lost the battle and let go. She felt in her heart that her life was ending.

Then suddenly Melody found that she was no longer drowning. Miraculously, she felt herself being pulled up toward the surface instead of down into the depths of the darkness she had been resisting. It was at this moment that she realized that several hands were now clutching her wrists, attempting to free her and returning her to safety.

As she thought back to that moment when she had let go, she was unsure of whether it was more a leap of faith or the inability to hold on any longer that had caused her to release the hold that she had on the tree. However, she was relieved to find that her brothers had circled back when they realized that she was in crisis. They were able to pull her from the undertow, and Melody's life was spared.

Unfortunately, this event had a negative effect on her from that day on, as she developed a tremendous fear of water. At that point, Melody lost all desire to participate in any water activities.

When she met Mike, she made this fear known to him relatively early on in their relationship. He was an outdoorsman, and float trips were among his favorite activities. Melody had wanted so desperately to spend time exploring life with him. So for the first few years, she tried to put her fears aside so she could experience his interests by his side.

In time, she confessed to Mike that water sports just weren't something she really enjoyed. He understood, as she knew he would. For several years, they found other ways to spend time together doing hobbies that they both enjoyed. When groups of friends would plan float trips, Melody would often participate in the camping and leave the floating part to the "water rats."

Melody recalled that last float/camping trip that they took together. She had discovered that everyone else had returned to the campsite while Mike's whereabouts seemed to be unaccounted for. His friends all knew of his canoeing abilities and felt sure of his safety, but her fear took hold as she awaited his return with sheer panic in her every thought.

A vicious storm had passed through just a few hours before, and she was afraid that he had fallen victim to that very same fast-moving water she had grown to fear all those years ago. She convinced his brother, along with his best friend, to drive her to their "take-out point." The sun had fully set and the moonlight was now his only remaining guide.

As they backed the truck from its parking spot near their tent, a drenched Mike came sauntering down the lane back toward the campsite. He had been waiting on a sandbar for a couple who had been floating with them to catch up, unaware that they had "taken out" at the halfway point and returned to the campsite long before. Once the storm passed, he was able to continue on in his canoe with the hope that he just didn't see them pass by.

Fortunately, when he arrived at the final destination along the muddy banks, an employee from the canoe rental establishment just happened to be passing by. With her help, he loaded the canoe onto the vehicle and was driven back to the safety of a dry tent and a warm fire, as well as to Melody's ecstatic arms.

A few years before Mike's death, he found a way to rekindle his love of the sport and included his children now as well. Mike, Joe, William, and even Christine began an annual ritual of a white-water rafting trip, along with a few very close friends, while Melody enjoyed a little "Grandma time" with Brooke. It was the best of both worlds—a true compromise that benefited everyone.

Due to her pregnancy, Christine opted out of the last trip that took place just two months before Mike's accident, and it turned out to be a great bonding experience for Mike with just his boys. While Mike would have loved for Christine to join them, it offered him a little father-son time with Joe and William, which gave him several stories to share upon their return. Melody could tell that he'd had the time of his life yet again. He had a way of experiencing life in a way that Melody could only dream about.

Why Melody hadn't learned that all-important lesson early on too she didn't know. But she now realized that life was most importantly about perception. She knew that it wasn't her floating accident that had restricted her for all of those years but the way she chose to react to it.

Mike had encouraged her to be a free spirit. It wasn't his way to hold her back. She recalled how he had always longed for her to reach for the stars; she was just too afraid to try. What if she failed? Now she realized that without him in her life to encourage her, she would have to encourage herself or stagnate.

Now that she only had her memories of him and the knowledge that he would never walk beside her again in this life, she was finding a new sense of courage. She was finally attempting to find the zest that had only been presented for her to see, not feel, in her earlier life. Melody now understood that it was her turn to find a way to experience living life to its fullest.

CHAPTER 10

Every Step of the Way

Now, not long after she had jumped back into home ownership, Melody learned the true meaning of the phrase "What doesn't kill you only makes you stronger." She recalled that feeling of loneliness and despair she had felt during the early months after Mike's death and saw that she had come a long way in the year since his accident.

In her mind she remembered how, in the first days of grieving, she would look out at what appeared to her as a huge backyard with animosity and fear. Melody had felt that she would never be able to tackle the chores that she had previously considered to be her own, much less try to overcome obstacles to perform the projects and responsibilities that Mike had taken on throughout their years together. It had been nearly thirty years since she had operated a lawnmower, and all of a sudden she had to figure it all out! He had taken such good care of her, providing for her every need. The truth of the matter was that he had taken care of her too well, and she now knew it. She recalled suddenly feeling lost—completely.

While she was planning her second move, Melody had initially considered purchasing a condominium, but after months of living in that small Indiana apartment, she had realized that she needed a bigger place to call her own. Amazingly enough, that is now what she had; and she knew it was where she belonged. However, at first that wounded bird that Mike had seen in her all those years ago resurfaced. She hired a neighbor boy to mow the lawn and experienced the pitfalls of hiring several handymen before she finally got up the courage to make things work for herself.

With a little "encouragement" from a neighborhood cat, she began the amazing task of creating a masterpiece in her backyard. The previous owner once had an aboveground swimming pool, and the sand that was left behind attracted nearby felines. Melody knew that something had to be done; her dogs would not allow such behavior to continue. Truth be told, the presence of the cat waste in her yard was causing Angel and Hogan to become ill. She had to take action. So she explored her creativity and designed a patio in her mind to be built in its place.

One of Melody's ways of coping in her times of deep sorrow was by reaching out to people by means of various types of social media. Once she created this patio in her mind, she asked for help online in the construction process. No one seemed to pay attention to her request, and she had no takers. So Melody began the build alone. Occasionally a neighbor would see her struggling while hauling a load of lime or rock out to her backyard and would offer a hand. But for the most part, she created this relaxing space all on her own. And 13 tons of lime, 155 patio tiles, and 60 bags of river rock later, Melody was the owner of a patio that she was sure would have made her late husband proud.

Once the project was completed and the first fire was built in the pit, Melody realized that she had learned to trust her abilities and now felt that she could reach for the stars. In time, she bought a lawnmower and supplies, and she completed several other landscaping projects on her own. While at first she was rather discouraged by the lack of offers for assistance, she now beamed with pride at her accomplishments. Her home with its new embellishments would be a place where friends, family, and anyone else in the neighborhood who just longed to stay warm on a chilly evening would congregate for years to come.

It didn't take long, though, for Melody to realize just how awesome her neighbors could be. She developed strong friendships and soon found that she had several people close by whom she could rely on whenever help was warranted. Sometimes it was tempting for her, but she kept her mind on her initial objective, not allowing herself to become too dependent upon anyone.

She now knew that she could jump over any hurdle that got in her path; she just had to put her mind to it. It was then that she learned to believe in herself in the same way Mike had believed in her for all of those years.

He had cheered her on and encouraged her for so long, but she had never taken the time to see herself through his eyes until now. She had gained a whole new perspective on life, and she was able to see herself as the amazing woman Mike had always insisted she was. When she looked deep within, Melody discovered great potential and strength.

She had grown a lot through the course of that first year in her new home, and she continued to learn more and more about herself as time marched on. Despite her grief and sorrow over her loss, she never felt alone again. Melody knew that Mike's spirit was with her every step of the way.

CHAPTER 11

She Would Overcome

Over the course of the initial years of her grief journey, Melody had grown to realize just how much she actually loved to travel. Whenever her grief became too much for her to bear alone, she booked a flight or gassed up her car and spent time with someone she rarely got the chance to see, generally whomever had been on her mind the most. She discovered that an early pattern had been formed, but it seemed to work well for her. Melody had become very in tune with her inner self.

It seemed as though she was now experiencing so much more than she had ever imagined, and at times the guilt of her newfound life became more than she could bear. In time, she began to realize that it was not in spite of Mike, but because of him that she now lived life so fully. She found herself participating in activities that she would have never done when Mike was alive. At first, this concerned her. She wondered about the point where grief's journey had brought her and what the implications might be.

One day when she was feeling even more adventurous than usual, it became clear to her that while she did not have a death wish, she also no longer feared death. She knew that a great love awaited her on the other side. With this knowledge, she had found the strength to embrace life completely.

It was about this same time that she found a new hobby. She laced up her old but hardly worn tennis shoes. When traveling just didn't seem practical, she could simply put one foot in front of the other and walk as life unfolded before her eyes. Suddenly she began seeing sights as if for the first time, and inspiration for the day often would appear from virtually anywhere. Her muse ranged from a butterfly landing on a poison ivy plant, a dog that approached her from nowhere with his little tail wagging, or the beauty of a tree changing colors as the seasons passed.

One particular day as her feet hit the pavement, Melody's mind began to wander back to the life she had so reluctantly left behind just years before. She realized that while she refused to live her life in the past, she occasionally had to look back to see just how far she had come.

She recalled a memory that, at the time, had seemed unpleasant. But now it made her see Mike's love more than she had comprehended at the time. It had been just a month before his accident, and he had returned early that morning from his usual route. Hearing his footsteps on the floor above their bedroom, she got out of bed and headed toward the staircase to greet him. By the time she reached the top of the stairs, however, he had already ventured out to water the fruit trees he had recently planted for her. Angel and Hogan were out with him for their morning run and had plopped themselves at his feet when she stepped onto the back porch dressed only in a nightshirt. She wished him a quick good morning and then returned inside only to feel an itch on her back. With an arm reaching behind her, she attempted to scratch when suddenly she felt a sharp sting from within her gown. A wasp had flown inside when she stepped out the door. Her initial reaction was to rip the garment off. With that, a now very angry wasp was flying overhead. In response to her fear, she opened the back door to their fortunately secluded backyard and yelled, "Mike, come quick!" Melody witnessed her fifty-year-old husband running faster than she had ever seen. He attended to her wounds that by this time had begun to make her back stiffen, and she was having difficulty coping with the pain. Mike applied ice to the sting, which happened to be directly on her scar from the back surgery she'd had just one year prior. Once he knew she was somewhat comfortable enough to be left alone, he ran down to the local pharmacy to purchase medication for the sting. He returned and applied it to the affected area and then sat with her for a while.

During their conversation, Melody commented on how quickly he'd come to her aid. He smiled the same smile she had seen from him when they were hardly more than teenagers, with a twinkle in his eye and a chuckle in his voice, and said, "When the wife of twenty-three years stands at the back door naked and yells, 'Mike, come quick,' *you run*!" During that final month of his life, she would smile every time she thought of his response that day in early July. But nothing could compare to the feeling she would get now, more than two years later when he was no longer in her world. Oh, how she missed him!

Suddenly tears began to well up in the corners of her eyes as she realized that, with the flip of just a few more pages on the calendar, she would be left to face a date that both she and Mike had held dear. They had vowed to love each other forever. She just didn't know that their forever would end so soon.

Now her reality was that once the Christmas presents were unwrapped and the leftovers from holiday festivities were put away, she would be left to celebrate their twenty-fifth wedding anniversary alone. The party supplies, wrapped in their boxes, still awaited the anniversary party that now had no reason to be held. She thought back to her wedding day and past anniversaries and the wonderful memories they'd shared during their too few years together.

She recalled that their wedding had been a simple but memorable affair. Mike and Melody both had agreed that it was about a marriage, not a wedding. They had become engaged and just three weeks later, rings and vows were exchanged. The wedding party consisted of the couple and two witnesses, Mike's brother and Melody's best friend. This had set the tone for their life together. The newlyweds spent their days (and nights) living for one another and taking care of each other.

Melody looked back at the much simpler time when she and Mike were merely beginning their lives together all those years ago. She recalled a bachelorette party that consisted only of her and her maid of honor, Elaine. But she also recalled that it was an evening of mischief and laughter—something these two had spent years together perfecting. The truth of the matter was that Melody wouldn't have had it any other way. She could think of no better way to spend her final night as a single woman.

At the same time, Mike was celebrating his last night of "bachelorhood," sitting at a poker table with several buddies. Thinking back to that night, Melody's mind recalled a late-night phone call from Mike's best friend. Apparently, the groom-to-be had expressed a desire to come home but was in no condition to get himself there without her assistance. Melody and Elaine discovered an interesting sight when they arrived at their destination just minutes later. An extremely intoxicated Mike was sitting upright at the poker table, and much to their amusement, they found that he was still winning. That was the first and last time Melody would ever find Mike letting himself get to that state. He liked maintaining control of his surroundings. She chalked it up to his anxiety about the events of the upcoming day. She knew that before she had come into his life, he had no intention of ever being anything other than a confirmed bachelor. Melody had changed his mind, and it really hadn't taken her long to accomplish this task. In all of their years together that followed, Mike never showed the least sign of regret for their decision.

Now, twenty-five years later, the bride was left to celebrate the occasion alone. Melody knew that she had to learn how to view dates on the calendar as merely numbers on paper, but this wasn't an easy task for her. She had grown to learn that acknowledging an obstacle was always the first step in getting beyond it, and Melody knew this would be no different. Maybe not yet, but in time she would overcome.

CHAPTER 12

Just His Way

After two years of grieving, it seemed that the problem of not sleeping and dreaming had replaced itself with a much deeper problem for Melody. She now found herself with the burden of dreaming too much, and it had become quite painful for her. These dreams included a range of characters, but the basic subject was always relatively the same. In the dreams, the people she cared most about were contacting her and asking her to keep out of their lives. She suddenly felt that initial feeling of loneliness once more—multiplied tenfold. But this time she had no clue where to turn. So she picked up a pen and began putting words on paper. She began to understand that sometimes you just have to look through the moment and explore the possibilities.

For many years, Mike had told her that she needed to write, but she never listened until he was gone. Suddenly it was as though there was a force ripping at her heart, making her see her true potential. Why had she never felt this side of herself before?

It was as though Mike's voice, which now only existed in her heart, was speaking directly to her, saying, "Get your heart off of your sleeve and find out your capabilities. Discover yourself for who you really are. It is time for you to see yourself as I have seen you!" It was as though Mike was speaking to her in a way unlike anything she had ever experienced. She had always had an artistic quality about her, but she felt that this was a far reach even for her.

Growing up, music had been her passion. At one time she even entertained the notion of a career in the field. But family life redirected that focus very early in her life, and she had never looked back. Melody recalled just two years before his death when she found a desire to reconnect with "musical friends" from her past. She had traveled the country, performing with this musical group during her teenage years. It wasn't that she had necessarily been trying to hide the creative side of herself from Mike; she had just never felt the need to introduce him to her former world until this particular stage in their life. With love and support, Mike stood patiently by her side as she planned a thirtieth reunion for a group of people whom he had never met, people who had meant everything to her before she knew him.

The reunion was a huge success. Mike wasn't a performer, but he had developed a strong connection with music during his life as well. He watched from the sidelines with camera in hand, recording every moment of the day for Melody. Mike always seemed to support her in whatever grabbed her attention at the moment. He knew that she had a need to explore and expand her mind. He would have done anything for her, and she knew it! Just one year after this reunion, he would prove this to her in ways she never would have imagined, when her injuries from the automobile accident several years before would reach a point that she could no longer tolerate. When life seemed to drag her down, he was right by her side, ready to pick her up. That was just his way.

CHAPTER 13

A Love Like No Other

Melody often looked back upon her daily life with Mike. She realized that during their years together, it had seemed to her that they had lived a modest and somewhat uneventful life. In her eyes, it was just an average life. The speed bumps they had encountered throughout their lifetime together had always left her trying to keep her chin up, but she never realized what she had until it was gone. This was something that became overwhelmingly apparent to her almost immediately upon Mike's death. How could she have been so blind to life and love?

At times, the guilt became extremely insurmountable for her. She hoped that Mike too realized how strong her love for him had been and still was. She did not question his love for her. Seeing herself through his eyes gave her a perspective that she would never have paid attention to when he walked by her side.

Melody remained fully aware that their love had not died when the crash occurred, and she felt a sense of desire and obligation to make sure that the people who had been a part of his life knew how much they had meant to him and how unfortunate were those who never got the chance to know him. So with pen in hand, she began to relive their years together to share their love story with the world or at least anyone who cared to read.

She reflected back to a steamy day in August when the inspiration first seemed to hit her, just days after her life had begun feeling so incomplete. In an effort to find Mike's spare keys, she was cleaning out his junk drawer in their kitchen. She happened upon the greeting card he had given her just months before he had died. The front cover was adorned with beautiful sparkling pink roses in full bloom with the words "For My Wife" across the middle. She slowly and somewhat reluctantly opened the front cover. She had no memory of the contents within. After the shock she'd felt that night when the earth-shattering knock at her front door had happened, her memory had failed her more times than she cared to count. She wasn't even sure if she had kept the card safely tucked away or if this was something Mike had done for her. Due to its location, she suspected the latter. Suddenly she encountered an outburst of mixed emotions. She felt so loved but so sad! With a tear in her eye, she began to read some of the last sentimental, sweet words he had expressed to her. Melody knew more than ever before that even though the words on this card were someone else's, the thoughts and feelings were 100 percent Mike's. As she peered through her tears, she read on and at times could even hear his voice reading along with hers as she clutched this keepsake in her hands:

You've heard that saying, "a man of few words." And that's me—a man of almost no words at all, especially when I want to say how important you are to me, how much I love you.
You deserve to hear that every day because the simple truth is you're the best wife a guy could have.
Happy Mother's Day
Love, Mike

Although these words were expressed to her prior to his death, they hadn't meant nearly as much as when she discovered this card just weeks after he died. Melody was overcome once more with the memory of a love so strong it could surpass the test of distance and time. She knew that she had been truly loved unconditionally.

It suddenly became clear to her that theirs was a love unlike anything she had ever felt before or would ever feel again. She remembered the talks they'd shared about growing old together, about waiting on the front porch in rocking chairs with anticipation and joy for the grandchildren to arrive someday, hopefully bringing great grandchildren to visit. Melody realized that these were now memories that would never be created—at least not with Mike. Sometimes the pain seemed like too much for her to deal with, and once more she had to redirect her focus as she had done years before when she had implemented her fifteen-minute rule.

In time the pain had lessened, but it certainly never went away. She had become comforted by the fact that they had shared a love so strong that it still kept her warm on those cold winter nights, now that her arms were left feeling empty. Melody realized that Mike would be waiting someday with "Open Arms" to greet her when her time on this Earth came to a close.

Melody certainly didn't perceive herself as a grief expert by any means. However, people had told her that she seemed to have a refreshing perspective toward the journey of grief than others, and many other widows she encountered during those initial years had expressed that it was as if she were reading their minds, and speaking the words they only wished they'd had the ability to say.

She found it therapeutic to allow her fingers to stroke the keys of her laptop. Inspiration hit at awkward times, and Melody even had to retreat from her everyday activities periodically. But she knew it was what she needed to do, so she did!

Throughout her grieving process, Melody had developed the ability to find something positive in nearly everything she encountered. At times, this was more challenging than almost anything she had ever attempted. She realized now, reflecting back, that even the wasp sting had become a memory she had grown to cherish. If she could put a positive spin on that event, Melody could find a silver lining in virtually anything.

She realized that memories were all she really needed, and she could fall back on them whenever a pick-me-up was necessary. This was an insight she wished she'd had when Mike was still here and they could have created more memories together, but now she just had to make the best of the life she had been left to live.

As a middle-aged widow, Melody came to understand that she had a different perspective on life and love than many of her peers. Watching other couples taking their special someone for granted was at times more than she could bear, and she just had to pull back in order to keep from even telling stangers just how lucky they truly are. She knew that tomorrow wasn't anything to take for granted. It was a gift that should always be appreciated. After all, hers had been ripped away without warning.

Melody realized that if she could impart any wisdom upon those around her, it was this: never skim over life and love. Appreciate what you have and make sure those in your life realize just how important they are to you. Self-expression gets easier with practice and is very rewarding at the end of the day. Love isn't something that you should ever have to look for, but a strong and lasting relationship is something that you have to work together to achieve.

Melody could only hope that somewhere down the road ahead in her life, a love just half as fulfilling as what she had with Mike would happen to her once more. She realized that a "kitchen stranger" wasn't likely to land in her life ever again. Melody knew that a love like that would most likely never show itself in her life again at this stage, but she would be OK. Melody was prepared to walk life's path with just her memories of what Mike had given her. Theirs was a love like no other.

CHAPTER 14

Open Arms

One day Melody found her mind traveling back to that special weekend she'd shared with Mike just days before she'd lost him.

Melody recalled her attentive husband putting her needs above his own as he often did. She envisioned herself riding in the passenger seat of their family car as he drove them past the very same mile marker along the highway where she would soon find herself placing fresh-cut flowers in honor of his memory. Although she hadn't been anywhere near the scene of his accident on that fateful night, her mind still periodically focused on her beloved and what he must have gone through in those final hours.

She reminisced of how, during their trip, the mix CD he'd created the evening before rang out through the speakers, and she took for granted the thoughts and feelings he'd had when he compiled the songs. As time proved, these very same songs would become important to her, as if they were messages from above, from his heart directly to hers now that she could no longer hear his voice aloud.

Melody recalled many of the conversations they'd had during their three-hundred-mile journey that Saturday morning, as they drove to meet up with family members whom she hadn't seen in so long, and looking back, she wished that her focus had been a little more on him and less on them.

Melody now searched the vault that her memory had become with thoughts of the events of their final days together. She recalled that once they arrived at the hotel where her niece's wedding was scheduled to be held, her enthusiasm had begun to be somewhat shadowed by her fatigue. She had worked an evening shift on this particular night and they had left on their trip almost immediately after she had ended her workday. This did not allow her any time to sleep. The excitement had kept her from the intended plan—for her to sleep during the ride. Mike witnessed her body winding down probably more than even Melody herself had noticed.

He stood by her side every moment of the day as they attended their niece's wedding and other festivities together. Mike had been holding a camera in his hands but found a way to grasp hers lovingly as the minister guided the young couple through their vows and especially when they stated the phrase that Melody would soon find grabbing onto her so tightly in the days to follow: "Till death parts us." She had no idea that her vows were about to end so abruptly just a couple of days later. If she'd had any idea at all, Melody would never have released Mike's grasp. She knew that if she could have, even years later, she would be holding on still.

She thought more about the day and how they had laughed hysterically at a conversation that had taken place as they had awaited the newlyweds' arrival at the reception. Melody recalled how the sound of their roaring laughter had caught the attention of many of the surrounding tables, as if they had been dancing on their table or something equally entertaining.

Soon the bride, Marie, and her new husband appeared and dinner was served. Melody's eyes became heavier as time went on. Mike, who had always seemed to be so tuned in to her needs, knew that she would not be able to remain at the reception much longer. At one point, he disappeared briefly for what she thought was a trip to the restroom.

Once the serving tables were moved and the dance floor was cleared, the music began to play. After the father-daughter dance, the DJ summoned all married couples upon the dance floor. The purpose of this dance was to discover which couple in attendance had been married the longest. With twenty-three years behind them, Melody and Mike lasted longer than many, but several couples still remained upon their dismissal.

Melody had staggered to the dance floor at Mike's request. She knew that he would want at least one dance with her. As with so many aspects of their relationship, their moments spent on the dance floor were always about nothing but the two of them. In their eyes, they were the only ones in the room as their feet moved to the beat. Never before had an occasion presented itself that Mike wouldn't find a way to put his loving arms around her waist and pull her in close as their song played. With a touch of sadness, Melody felt that this would be an exception to their rule. She felt as though she had no strength left, and she planned to excuse herself as they left the dance floor to make her way to their room just floors above, to a bed that had been screaming her name for the better part of the day.

With that in mind, Melody reminded Mike of her need for rest. Mike empathetically suggested that she wait with him long enough to offer one last congratulations and goodnight to the happy couple. She agreed, and they stood together at the edge of the dance floor until the end of this special dance. The back of her substantially smaller frame rested comfortable against his chest as he held her tired body upright. As the bride and groom exited the dance floor, she expressed her well wishes and was about to turn to walk out the door when a familiar sound and the clutching grasp of her soul mate pulled her back out to the middle of the dance floor once more.

Melody realized that the love of her life hadn't excused himself earlier for any other reason than to speak to the man in charge of the music. Mike had apparently informed him that his wife had been fighting off total exhaustion after traveling all morning with no sleep, following a hard night at work just hours before. Mike told the DJ that they had never attended an event where they didn't dance to the song that reminded them of when their love was new a couple of decades ago. He asked that their song be played as soon as possible upon completion of the customary dances.

Now, as a widow, Melody thought about that weekend, and the one feeling that stuck most vividly in her mind was the memory of her head resting on Mike's chest and the strength of his arms wrapped tightly around her. Melody realized that he was her sense of strength as her tired body barely moved, and she knew that that was where she belonged. He was the one who had made her world complete. He had been her strength right up until the end of his time on Earth.

Now that he was gone, she held tightly to the memories they had created, and she longed for the day when her spirit would arrive at their eternal home, where she would meet him again and he would be awaiting her arrival for yet another dance—with open arms.

A Note from the Author

At the end of the first year of my grieving process, with much encouragement but little confidence, I enrolled in a writing class at a local community college. During this course, my instructor gave me a little advice. He stated that two of my essays definitely warranted consideration for sharing with the world. With that in mind, I give you chapter 1, "A Widow's Prison," as well as my conclusion, a perspective on the five stages of grief.

May these words offer you encouragement when life causes you to travel this path or the opportunity to appreciate more fully a love that you have not yet lost.

It seems that love and the grief it leaves behind are a loop. Much like a wedding band, they appear to have no beginning or ending. Pain lessens in time, but what it leaves behind creates emotions that at times take a strong hold on those of us left here to feel them.

Conclusion
The Five Stages of Grief

Anyone who has ever dealt with the death of a loved one can most likely name the typical five stages of grief. These stages were identified originally in a 1969 book titled *Death and Dying* by Elisabeth Kübler-Ross. Those individuals who have traveled down grief's path would also tell you that they do not come in any given order, and neither do you visit with each stage just once during the process. Sometimes these stages fade in and out so subtly that even grief's participants find it difficult to identify their current stage. As my own grief process indicates, each individual grieves differently. My observations are merely that—mine.

Often *denial* is the first stage recognized in a grief situation. Many times those who have never experienced this stage may get it confused with disbelief. That is not really what I've discovered denial to be about. I prefer to look at it as a sort of "numbing." When I heard the news about my husband's accident, it had physical implications. Elevated blood pressure and heart rate were the most predominant reactions that

I encountered almost immediately. I now realize that was my body's method of protection, giving me something else to think about. Before my experience, I looked at this stage with the understanding that it only entailed disbelief.

As the police officers began to inform me of my husband's accident, they dispatched paramedics to my home as well. So many of the hours and days following seem to be vague and consist of scattered memories. This has become my discovery of the stage known as denial. I actually found this experience to cause a sense of euphoria. It seemed as if nothing could touch me now—life already had left me numb.

For many, *anger* proceeds denial. Frequently it is indicated that this stage targets not only the departed individual but also a higher power. Many search for answers only to find that none really exist. In my case, I not only wrestled with the whys of the situation but also the hows. My husband's death left me with far too many unanswered questions, and until I reached the acceptance stage, anger prevailed. I found anger to be a gripping stage, and it affected my feelings toward many individuals in my life for quite a while. I recall having conversations with family members, expressing my anger about him leaving me. Their response was almost always the same, "You shouldn't be angry with him. He didn't mean to leave you." While I knew that to be true, the emotions were still present. "How can you be returning to normal life while I sit here brokenhearted?" was the biggest anger hurdle I had to jump. Within days family and friends resumed their daily routine while I couldn't even look a clock square in the face. In time I did find a way to rejoin the human race, but it didn't happen overnight. As time went on, I found myself reflecting on the funeral and feeling hurt by individuals who failed to attend the service or even just contact me to express sympathies. While some of these emotions may have been warranted, others were not.

The most obscure stage for me was *bargaining*. It wasn't about asking God to bring him back to me. It was about helping me through the tough days I was encountering. I found it to be a time of deep introspection and faith seeking. I attended church faithfully in hope that I would find a way to cope with my new life.

In many ways, I feel that bargaining and denial are closely related. I found myself wondering if this was really just a bad dream. Would I wake up to realize that it was just that? I also remember asking God to bring him back. I would have done anything to see that happen. I knew it wasn't realistic, but it didn't stop me from asking. Although many books on grief categorize this as bargaining, I can't help but feel that it wanders closely to the denial stage as well.

Depression for me was more a sense of loneliness and possibly even boredom. I missed my husband with all of my heart and knew that nothing was going to bring him home again. I hit this stage quickly and refused to let it take over my life. I sold our family home and moved to a strange town two hundred miles away from almost everyone I knew. I realized that life was going to have to start again for me, and I was going to tackle it head on. Just three months after I lost the love of my life, I packed up a handful of belongings and moved into a one-bedroom apartment, along with my two dogs. Looking back, I realize that it was probably the best thing I could have done to get through that stage. I was able to leave those memories behind when five months later my dream home practically fell into my lap. All of those lonely nights of crying and longing for what could never be again were left behind, and the next chapter began to write itself.

The final, but certainly not the least important, stage is *acceptance*. I vividly remember feeling that this would be a stage I would never enter. It seemed as though it would mean that I felt OK with what had happened, as if the loss was a good thing. I now see, having survived the entrance into this stage, that it is not the case. Acceptance in its simplest form means that it has become possible to merely find my smile again. While a temporary smile would cross my face from time to time even early in the grieving process, it was only a sign that I might reach acceptance someday. In time, with the help of various great people who have become active participants in my life, this stage has become a reality. Although I still meander back to previous stages occasionally, I find myself residing mostly within the fifth stage of acceptance.

I had a few advantages over many suffering with the affliction of grief. When I clocked out of my office, just hours before his accident occurred, it was the last time I was on the time clock, at least for that first year. I quit my job and took all of the time I needed to work through some very strong emotions. I wrote about them often as well. I began writing a blog, expressing my deepest emotions with hopes that someone would read them and find their own sense of comfort. Writing for me was very cathartic. It was my therapy. I also had many hands reaching out to grab mine. Some belonged to friends, but many belonged to strangers. I was selective about which hands I reached back toward, but I have developed new bonds and reestablished a few old ones along the way. It's been an adventure, but that's what life is all about. After more than two years of grieving, I am living my life again with a whole new appreciation for things I previously took for granted. In many ways, the grieving process has made my life a much richer experience. It taught me how to enjoy food more, smile more broadly, and laugh more loudly. Although I don't care to go through the process ever again, I know that is unrealistic. But I also know that I can get to the other side and may walk out of it as a better person. Grief gave me something I never would have expected to find along this journey—a new perspective on life.

About the Author

Melissa Simmons grew up on a dairy farm in Illinois. She is the youngest of four children and was raised to appreciate family life.

After a failed relationship left her to raise her young son alone, she found trust something that was hard to come by. But when Andy walked into her world on that breezy April night, everything changed for her.

The couple spent twenty-five wonderful years together, exploring life and love before Andy was killed in a tractor–trailer accident.

During the years before Andy's death, he had tried to convince Melissa to write a book, but she resisted. Once she grasped the reality of her new life, the motivation hit her, and the words you just read came flowing from her fingers, with every stroke on the keyboard.

Although she cried many tears during her grief journey, Melissa feels that she is a much-stronger individual now, knowing that she was loved so deeply.

After just a few short months of recovery, living in close proximity to her children, Melissa ventured out into the big, beautiful world alone and purchased a home in a small, rural community. She currently resides there with her two dogs, Dottie and Maxwell, and enjoys brief visits with her children and grandchildren whenever possible.

Through her journey of loss and self-discovery, she has learned a new way of looking at life, finding beauty in things she never noticed before.

Although her heart still aches for Andy, she has learned to use his love for her as a source of strength. There is no mountain too high or river too wide to keep her from feeling his never-ending love for her.

Made in the USA
San Bernardino, CA
13 November 2014